Copyright 2007 Jennie E. Nicassio
Rocky
The Rockefeller Christmas
Author, Jennie Nicassio
Illustrator, Dina Colangelo
Manufactured in the United States. Published by Nieje Productions LLC

NIEJE
Productions LLC

Foreword

Since 1997, the lighting of the Rockefeller Christmas has been broadcast live, to hundreds of millions, on NBC's Christmas in Rockefeller Center telecast on a Wednesday after Thanksgiving. An estimated 125 million people flock to see the attraction each year. The Rockefeller Christmas tree is selected each year in November based on its heartiness and for its Christmas tree shape as well as its ability to support the heavy ornaments. The head gardener of Rockefeller Center and his team visit nurseries throughout the tri-state area while keeping his eye out for one-of-a-kind backyard trees. The hunt for the following year's tree begins more than a year in advance. Since 1931— when construction workers building Rockefeller Center put up a tree — locals and tourists alike have flocked to midtown Manhattan to bask in its glow and get into the yuletide spirit. The tree is erected in mid-November and lit in a public ceremony in late November or early December. The tree, usually a Norway spruce 69 to 100 feet tall, has been a national tradition each year since 1933. The Christmas Tree Lighting takes place late November and the tree remained on display until early January.

https://en.wikipedia.org/wiki/Rockefeller_Center_Christmas_Tree

Deep within the secret forest, past the Grove of the Grumpy Oaks, chubby chipmunks and squirrels busily gathered nuts for the long winter months ahead.

Reindeer practiced jumping over snowdrifts, hoping to pull Santa's sleigh this year. Excitement filled the forest because it was time to choose the Rockefeller Christmas Tree~

~and Little Rocky couldn't wait!

Rocky wasn't the biggest or the strongest. He was quite the opposite. He was a Norway Spruce. Unlike any other spruce, his branches were bare and bent the wrong way, his needles were hardly ever green.

Still, he longed to be the Rockefeller Christmas Tree.

The animals made fun of Rocky for his
seemingly impossible dream.

AJ, the squirrel, circled Rocky and
sang, "You're limp and bare; you'll never
be the Rockefeller Christmas Tree!"

As she combed her hair and admired her reflection in her mirror, Mrs. Pickles, the skunk, said, "What makes you think you can be the grandest tree for the world to see?"

Rocky lifted his branches and lowered his top as the skunk walked away. Tears ran down his twisted branches.

Rocky nodded off to sleep that night, away from the other animals, as marshmallow-sized snow began to fall.

Gusts of wind howled through the forest and shook Rocky's branches.

zzzz

The tallest tree appeared, and high in the branches sat AJ the squirrel.

In a booming voice, the tree asked, "I heard you're going to enter the Rockefeller Christmas Tree Contest?"

"Uh...yes," his voice trembling.
"Who are you?" Rocky said, looking
up at the huge tree.

"The name's Spruce, Bruce Spruce," the burly tree said
as he tipped his top and held out his branches.

"Between you and me, you don't have a chance. You're sure to lose~not that I have anything to worry about by the looks of you."

"Yeah, Rocky, withdraw your name," AJ added, trying to copy Bruce's bossy tone in his squeaky, squirrelly voice.

"You don't scare me!" Rocky said.

"Leave Rocky alone, Bruce," a wee voice said from behind Rocky.

Rocky turned to see a little fairy hovering in front of Bruce's face. She shook her finger at Bruce as sternly as a delicate wood fairy can.

"Remember what I said, Rocky," Bruce Spruce said before he and AJ departed, laughing.

The fairy turned her attention to Rocky. "Hello! I'm Mary Louise, the Guardian of the Forest," she said, buzzing around Rocky.

"Bruce and AJ~they're full of hot air," the fairy said dancing, trying to make him smile.

"Are you an enchanted fairy? Will magic make me handsome and strong like Bruce Spruce and the mighty white pine?"asked Rocky.

"There is no such thing as magic. You just have to believe."

Good-bye for now!"
Mary Louise said.
Just as quickly as
the fairy appeared,
she was gone.

"Believe? That's what I'll do! I'll drink more water,
and grow tall and green!"

"Look at me!" Rocky yelled, his words echoing through the forest.

The more he believed in himself, the more his confidence grew and grew, and soon he appeared to be what he imagined.

BELIEVE!

The tiny tree imagined he had thick branches. Every day he would tell himself he was tall and fluffy and green.

Magically, things began to happen. The more Rocky believed, the more he became what he imagined.

His branches unfolded into lush, dark green branches, and he grew to twice his size. Rocky swayed proudly, gleaming.

However, his new found confidence made the animals suspicious.

Mrs. Pickles and AJ huddled in the forest.

"Have you seen Rocky? He's changed,"
Mrs. Pickles said.

"His branches reach the sky,"
AJ replied. "It must be magic."

"Yes," said Mrs. Pickles. "The
Guardian of the Forest must have
put a spell on him!"

"I better tell Bruce!"

By now, it was time for the contest. The trees practiced standing tall, all, except... Bruce Spruce.

He and AJ hid at the edge of the forest behind the shadows, watching Rocky.

Bruce spoke in his mighty voice, "You may be right, AJ... it's magic."

"You're going to lose now, huh, Bruce?" squeaked AJ.

"Bah! We must find a way to catch the fairy and make her change Rocky back."

"How will we do that?"

"We'll set a trap!"

The despicable duo schemed up a way to trap Mary Louise. Her tiny home of pebbles and dried leaves was nestled in the forest where Mary Louise made ornaments for the champion of the contest. Bruce made a net of twigs to trap the fairy.

When Mary Louise left to gather more supplies to make her ornaments, AJ bounced out with the net.

The powerful tree caught Mary.

"You used magic on Rocky! Change him back or when I come back I'm tearing down your house!".

"Magic!" Mary Louise giggled. "I did no such thing."

AJ held Mary Louise captive behind a mound of snow while Bruce entered the competition.

"There's no spell! I told Rocky to believe in himself and anything would be possible."

"That's all?"

"Yes, now put me down!"

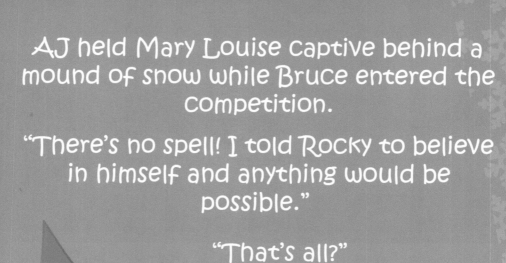

AJ freed Mary Louise, just in time to watch all the trees being judged.

ROCKEFELLER CHRISTMAS TREE CONTEST!!!!!

The judges flew overhead in helicopters, searching for the perfect tree. They inspected each tree and admired them as the trees drew themselves up to their full height.

But there was one tree that stood out from the rest. The tree they were looking at was Rocky!

"We found the perfect tree!" the judges shouted.

Rocky's branches were decorated with red ornaments and twinkling lights. Thousands gathered~even Bruce Spruce, AJ and Mrs. Pickles, who was still admiring herself in her mirror despite the amazing scene before her.

Mary Louise buzzed around Rocky one last time.

"Always remember: If you believe without a doubt and don't give up, you can do anything your heart desires!"

Mary Louise gave Rocky a wink and fluttered her wings. "See you in the North Pole with all the Rockefeller Christmas Trees from years gone by!" Rocky tipped his top, being careful not to drop his star, and raised a branch and waved goodbye. It was Rocky's happiest day!

The End

Dedicated to Louie, Mary, and Lori.

Forever in my heart

Gone but not Forgotten.

Bloopers

TRAIN LIKE ROCKY...

Praise for Rocky, The Rockefeller Christmas Tree

Heartwarming!

I just purchased this book to read in my special ed class because we needed something inspirational. Who could imagine that a book about a little tree, overcoming many obstacles to become the famous Rockefeller Christmas tree would inspire such great conversation amongst the student.
This book made us all smile because it is a fun read with a fabulous message to believe and follow your dreams... "The Little Train that Could" would be proud to share the Inspirational reading shelf with Rocky!

—Anonymous

Such a great story that inspires children to believe in themselves and achieve their dreams. Great book for my special needs son and all children!

—Michael G Pitacciato

Great Children's Story for the Holidays!

I just purchased this book for my six year old nephew, we were in need of something new for the holidays. This book is about a little tree, overcoming many obstacles to become the famous Rockefeller Christmas tree! This is a fun read that has a good message behind it "Follow your dreams" I recommend this children book as a great gift for your son/daughter, niece or nephew.

—Thomas Edgar

The most magical time of the year in New York City comes in November, with the lighting of the Rockefeller Christmas Tree. At that time, thousands of people from all over the world flock to the Big Apple in order to bear first-hand witness to the special holiday tradition. Because of the significance of the occasion, evergreens from all around the world dream of becoming the Rockefeller Christmas Tree, standing proudly at the center of the world stage for all to see – and young Rocky is no exception. The only problem? As a small, rather unattractive sapling, Rocky can barely compete with the more impressive, robust specimens seeking to steal the spotlight he so desperately craves; however, with a little help – and a strong belief in himself – Rocky may just see his long-held dream finally come true...

Rocky: The Rockefeller Christmas Tree is an enjoyable, heartwarming tale for readers of all ages. Touching on such universal themes as keeping the faith, believing in oneself, and persevering *through adversity, author Jennie Nicassio's inspiring story of overcoming the odds makes it* particularly appealing to young readers, providing them with invaluable life lessons that will serve them well for years to come. Furthermore, by crafting Rocky as a flawed, yet determined individual – rather than an immaculate, insuperable hero – Nicassio makes it easier for readers to relate to his passionate quest to succeed, despite the obstacles – both internal and external – standing in his way.

—Apex Review for Amazon

Rocky

Mary Louise

AJ

Bruce

Mrs. Pickles

The Magic in the Making

Stella and Rockefeller Tree

Christmas Magic Rockefeller Center

The first Rockefeller Christmas Tree

Memories

The first Rocky in 2009.

Photo's courtesy of:

Stella the Service Dog

"I'm living proof that not all medicine comes in a bottle"

https://www.facebook.com/StellaTheTherapyDog/?fref=ts

Clique Nova York Travel Agency

http://www.cliquenovayork.com/

Eclipse 2017

CPSIA information can be obtained
at www.ICGtesting.com
Printed in the USA
LVHW070735310520
657000LV00016B/151